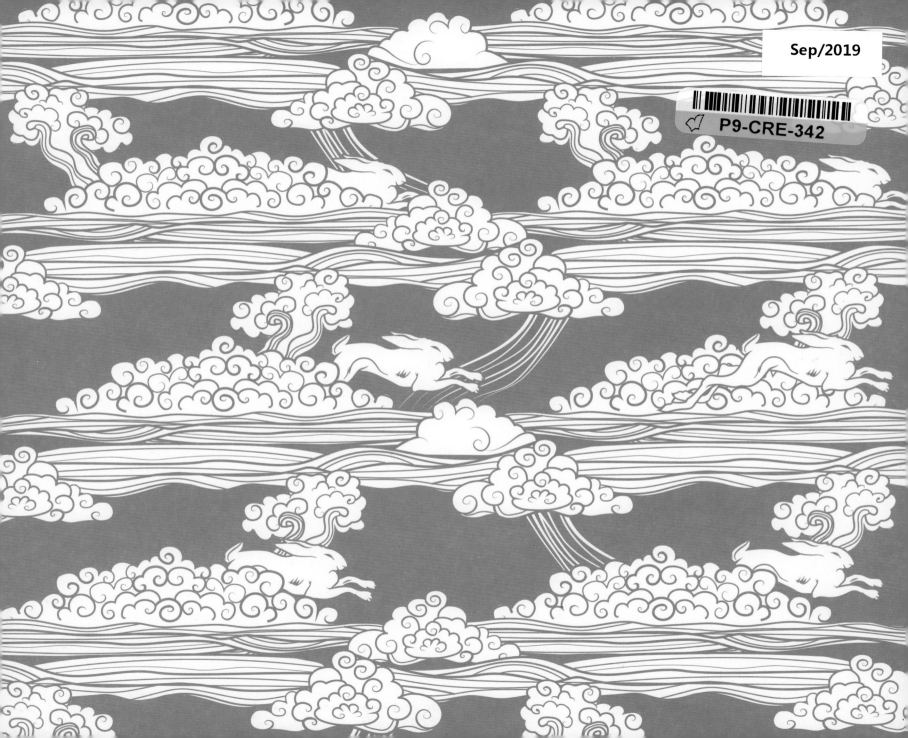

RABBIT NINJA

WORDS & PICTURES
BY
JARED TAYLOR WILLIAMS

DAVID R. GODINE, PUBLISHER
BOSTON

For Silas,
Because every night can't be noodle night
and sometimes our greatest battles are with ourselves.
I love being your dad.

First published in 2019 by
David R. Godine, Publisher, Inc.
Post Office Box 450
Jaffrey, New Hampshire 03452
www.godine.com

LIBRARY OF CONGRESS CATALOGING-IN-PUBLICATION DATA

Names: Williams, Jared T., author, illustrator
Title: Rabbit ninja / words & pictures by Jared T. Williams.
Description: Boston : David R. Godine, Publisher, 2018. | Summary: A young
rabbit imagines how much easier daily life would be if he were a ninja,
but he knows that sometimes, being himself is just fine. Includes facts about ninjas.
Identifiers: LCCN 2018016566 | ISBN 9781567926286 (hardcover : alk. paper)
Subjects: | CYAC: Ninja--Fiction. | Family life--Fiction. | Schools--Fiction. | Rabbits--Fiction.
Classification: LCC PZ7.1.W5463 Rab 2018 | DDC [E]--dc23
LC record available at https://lccn.loc.gov/2018016566

FIRST PRINTING, 2019
Printed in China

'Good morning little ninja.'

This is how my mother wakes me up in the morning.
This is because I always tell her how much better life would be if I were a ninja.

In real life, waking up is hard, and there are things to do
like brushing my teeth and getting dressed.

If I were a ninja, I wouldn't ever really sleep. I would just sit quietly on my remote mountainside, ever aware, ever watchful, and always ready.

In real life, I have to pack my backpack and eat my breakfast quickly, because if I don't hurry, I will be late for school.

If I were a ninja, I would silently eat my noodles,
stare at my sword, and think about being a ninja.

In real life, I have to rush to school,
put my things in my cubby, and sit down for opening circle.

If I were a ninja, I would carefully select my weapon
for the day's training and prepare to meet the other ninjas.

In real life, the school day is long, especially Mondays.
Though it helps when you get the answer right to the daily quiz.

If I were a ninja, I would show my Sensei exactly what it means
to be at one with my inner warrior…

In real life, recess is fun, but that's because I spend the whole time with my friends, pretending to be a ninja.

If I were a ninja, I wouldn't have to pretend.

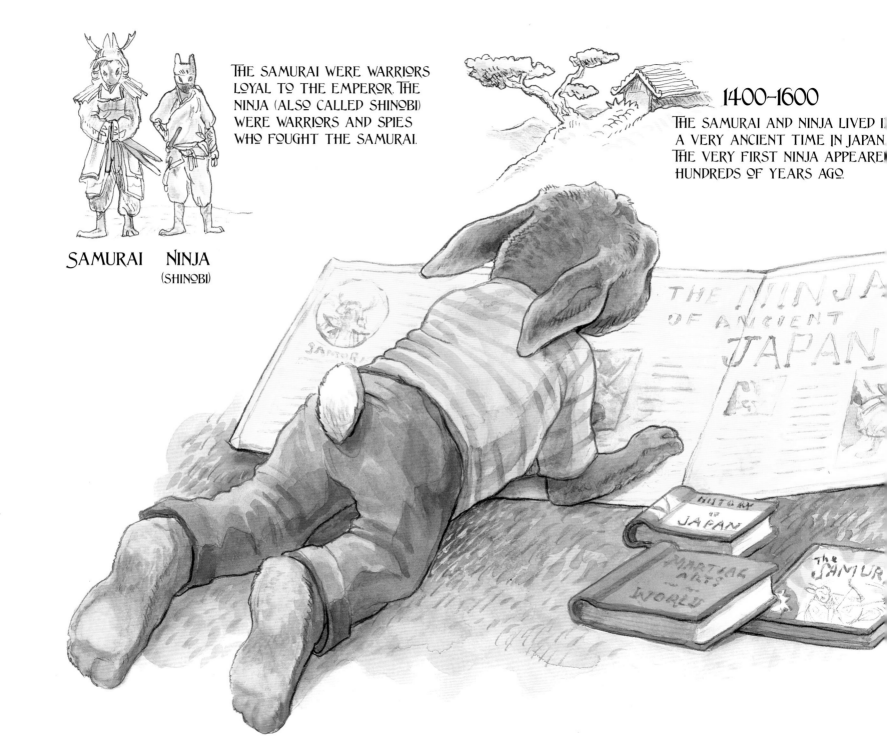

THE SAMURAI WERE WARRIORS LOYAL TO THE EMPEROR. THE NINJA (ALSO CALLED SHINOBI) WERE WARRIORS AND SPIES WHO FOUGHT THE SAMURAI.

SAMURAI NINJA
(SHINOBI)

1400-1600

THE SAMURAI AND NINJA LIVED IN A VERY ANCIENT TIME IN JAPAN. THE VERY FIRST NINJA APPEARED HUNDREDS OF YEARS AGO.

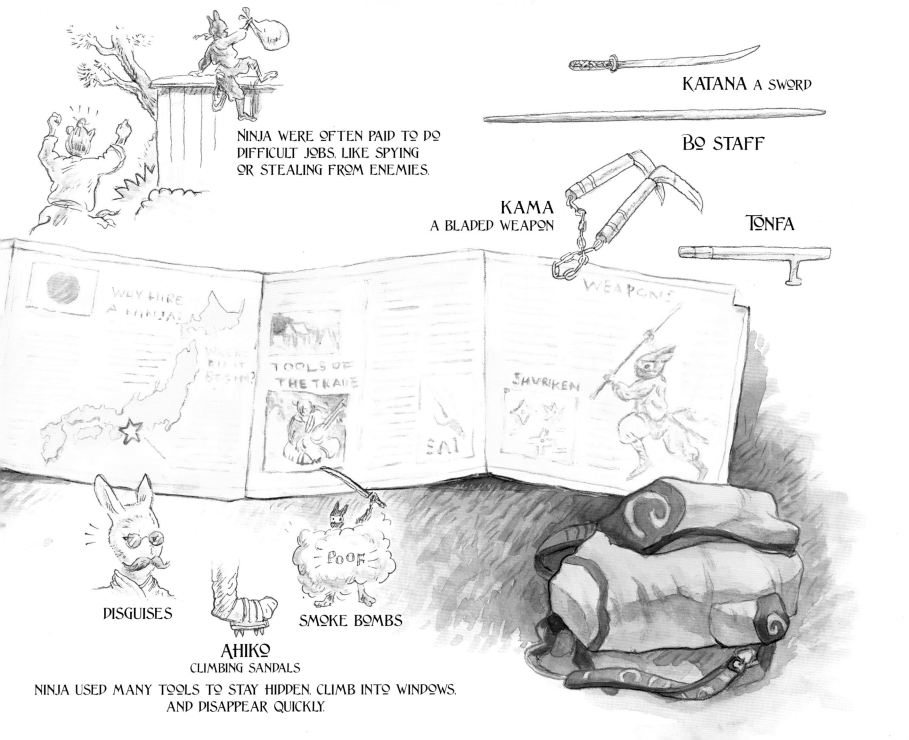

NINJA WERE OFTEN PAID TO DO DIFFICULT JOBS, LIKE SPYING OR STEALING FROM ENEMIES.

KATANA A SWORD

BO STAFF

KAMA
A BLADED WEAPON

TONFA

DISGUISES

AHIKO
CLIMBING SANDALS

POOF

SMOKE BOMBS

NINJA USED MANY TOOLS TO STAY HIDDEN, CLIMB INTO WINDOWS, AND DISAPPEAR QUICKLY.

In real life, walking home with dad is pretty fun.
And when I tell him I had a hard day, he tells me he has days like that too.

I'm not even sure ninjas have dads.

In real life, eating everything on my plate is hard. Except on radish nights.

If I were a ninja, I would concentrate and quietly eat my noodles.
Again.

In real life, bedtime always comes too soon, and I have to brush my teeth really well.

If I were a ninja, I would have enemies to defeat and no time for things like bedtime.

In real life, I'm almost never tired, but reading about ninjas helps.

A ninja must be quiet

quick   fast

strong   and brave.

But there are times when it's nice to be a little rabbit.

'Goodnight my little ninja.'